Turtle Tracks

By Sally Harman Plowden

Illustrated By Tee Plowden

Palmetto Conservation Foundation/PCF Press

Sponsored by Progress Energy

For Russell and our three girls: Caroline, Grace, and Anne. With love—S.H.P.
For my husband and our grandchildren—Charles, Caroline, Grace, and Anne—T.P.

Acknowledgements

The writer and artist would like to thank the following people for their interest and help: Carolyn Berry with Litchfield Books, Betsy Brabson and Jeff McClary with South Carolina United Turtle Enthusiasts, Dan Evans with the Caribbean Conservation Corporation, Sally Murphy and Joan Drew with the South Carolina Department of Natural Resources, Beth Caddell, Janet and Elizabeth Cotter, Sammie Sweeney Ferrigan, Kathy Creswell Murff, Lynn Floyd Wright, Barbara Stone, Ed Hadley, Sadie Jackson, Sara Cook, Daisy Harman, Harry Harman, Will, Sam, and Sarah Stormer, Charles Plowden, and especially Boots and Russell Plowden.

Edited by Yon Lambert
Design and layout by Sandy Husmann
Text Copyright © 2002 by Sally Harman Plowden
Illustrations Copyright © 2002 by Tee Plowden
Published by: Palmetto Conservation Foundation/PCF Press P.O. Box 1984 Spartanburg, S.C. 29304
www.palmettoconservation.org

10 9 8 7 6 5 4 3 2 1

Printed in Hong Kong by C&C Offset Printing Company, Ltd.

Library of Congress Cataloging-in-Publication Data
Plowden, Sally Harman, 1959-
 Turtle tracks / by Sally Harman Plowden ; illustrated by Tee Plowden.
  p. cm.
Summary: A girl vacationing with her family at the beach meets a volunteer who is helping newly-hatched loggerhead turtles to reach the water safely.

 ISBN 0-9679016-6-9

[1. Loggerhead turtle--Fiction. 2. Turtles--Fiction. 3. Beaches--Fiction.
4. Wildlife rescue--Fiction.] I. Plowden, Tee, 1935-ill. II. Title.
 PZ7.P7245 Tu 2001
 [Fic]--dc21
           2001001566

Dear Reader,

Progress Energy is extremely proud to sponsor its first children's book, Turtle Tracks.

Since our inception, Progress Energy has worked to serve as an exceptional corporate citizen in coastal communities across the Southeast. We award contributions to non-profit organizations primarily in support of education, economic development and the environment. For us, Turtle Tracks seems an especially appropriate partnership since it helps educate our children about the value of living in a larger ecosystem.

Our thanks to the Palmetto Conservation Foundation and the creators of Turtle Tracks — Sally Harman Plowden and Tee Plowden — for their commitment to loggerhead sea turtle conservation. By increasing public awareness and community participation, we can all work to strike a better balance between environmental quality and economic vitality on the coast.

Charles R. Wakild
Executive Director
Environment, Health & Safety

Every summer my family packs our blue van full of suitcases, beach chairs, buckets, and shovels for a trip to the beach. We have been going to the same gray beach house for as long as I can remember.

Our house has a screened porch facing the ocean where the grown ups sit in the evening and rock and talk.

In the corner of the porch is an old hammock. I like to play in it with my cousins. Sometimes we swing back and forth very fast. Other times, we sway slowly — listening to the screen doors opening and closing around us, as people go in and out to the beach.

W|hen we go to the beach, I always make sure to visit my aunt and uncle on an island down the coast.

Today, I am also going there to study a loggerhead turtle nest.

My aunt told me that about two months ago, a 300-pound mother turtle crawled out of the ocean, pulled herself along slowly with her flippers, and dug a hole in the sand to lay her eggs. Then she buried the eggs before returning to the water.

She will never know the baby turtles that have been hatching and climbing out of the nest for the past two nights. But today I hope to see at least one baby turtle. I have seen many animals at the beach but never a loggerhead turtle.

As my mother and I ride onto the island, I look for alligators in the marsh. Each summer, I have seen one in the very same spot – near the edge of the water, under an old popcorn tree limb. I see one there today, too. Just the tip of his snout and the top of his back and tail are showing.

As soon as we get to my aunt's house, I run around to the creek in her back yard.

My cousins and I have watched deer eat leaves from the trees along the banks of this creek. A blue heron also comes every day to sit on the post in the water. My aunt says the heron came during a hurricane a few years back. Before the storm, she had a dock in the creek behind her house.

Now, she has just four wooden posts.

And the blue heron.

In the late afternoon, my aunt joins us for our walk to the beach and the turtle nest. I wear my pink jelly shoes until we reach the sand so that I will not get splinters from the wooden walkway. As soon as we get to the beach, though, I take them off. I like to feel the warm sand and cool foamy water on my feet.

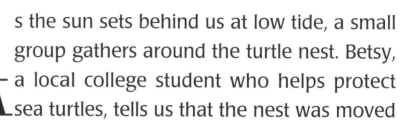

As the sun sets behind us at low tide, a small group gathers around the turtle nest. Betsy, a local college student who helps protect sea turtles, tells us that the nest was moved close to sand dunes to protect the eggs from high tides. "If seawater washes over the eggs too many times, it will destroy them," she says.

Most of these eggs have already hatched. The female turtles almost always lay their eggs at night, and their newly-hatched babies also choose the cool nighttime to push their way up and out of the nest. This evening, Betsy will count the eggshells and remove any hatchlings that might still be in the nest.

"Don't be too disappointed, though, if I don't find any live turtles," she warns. "The wire screen that we use to protect the nest keeps predators like foxes and raccoons away, but fire ants crawl right through it."

I wait impatiently and hope that Betsy finds a live loggerhead. Finally, I see her smile as she reaches into the nest and says, "We have some turtles."

She places three tiny, dark brown loggerhead hatchlings side-by-side on the hard, wet sand below the dune. Each turtle is about two-and-a-half inches long, smaller than my foot.

Betsy explains that the temperature determines whether the turtles will be boys or girls. "Because this summer has been so hot and dry," she says, "I think these babies must be girls."

I hope so. I imagine that the three hatchlings are my sisters and me, racing to the ocean on the first day of vacation.

"Crossing the sand is dangerous for the turtles," Betsy tells us. "They have flippers made for swimming, not walking on land. Sea turtles cannot pull their heads into their shells to protect themselves; and ghost crabs, sea gulls, foxes, raccoons, and dogs like to eat them."

Two of the hatchlings move quickly toward the water, but the third one lags behind. I am glad that we are there to protect her.

If we crowd too close to the loggerheads or move in front of them, though, Betsy makes us back away. Sea turtles move toward the brightest light — moonlight or, today, the sunlight shining on the ocean. Even my shadow thrown in front of the hatchlings could confuse them and make them turn in the wrong direction.

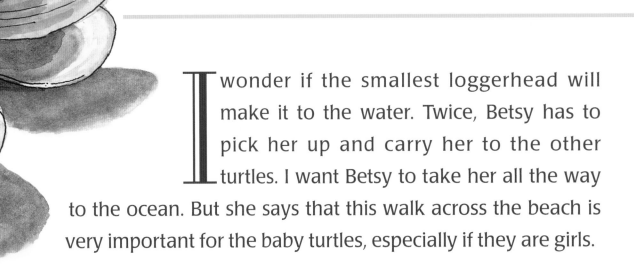

I wonder if the smallest loggerhead will make it to the water. Twice, Betsy has to pick her up and carry her to the other turtles. I want Betsy to take her all the way to the ocean. But she says that this walk across the beach is very important for the baby turtles, especially if they are girls.

"Scientists believe that years from now, one of these turtles may come back to this very beach and lay her eggs," Betsy explains. "Even if she swims more than 300 miles away, she will return to build her nest where she herself was hatched."

"How do sea turtles find their way back?" I ask.

"Scientists do not know for sure," Betsy tells us. "They think, though, that when a baby turtle first pulls herself across the sand as a hatchling she somehow imprints its texture and learns its smell and taste."

I scoop up a handful of sand and smell it as it falls through my fingers.

My parents know the way to the beach. So do my grandparents. Someone in my family has been coming to this part of the coast every summer for 180 years. For us, there are roads, signs, and people along the way to offer directions.

For turtles, the sand itself is a trail that I cannot see, smell, or feel.

As I watch for sea gulls or crabs that might eat these turtles, I notice another obstacle. The smallest hatchling goes headfirst into a footprint in the sand.

She flops down one side and gets stuck in the middle.

The group gathers around as she slowly struggles up the other side. Pulling, climbing, and sometimes slipping backwards, the hatchling reminds me of my baby sister when she was first learning to crawl.

This smallest loggerhead reaches the water last, but I am especially proud of her.

Like the other turtles, she has completed the first part of her journey. She will return to land only to lay her eggs, many years from now.

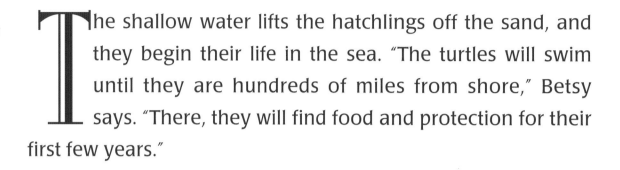

The shallow water lifts the hatchlings off the sand, and they begin their life in the sea. "The turtles will swim until they are hundreds of miles from shore," Betsy says. "There, they will find food and protection for their first few years."

I turn away from the ocean and see turtle tracks in the sand. Three lines that look like tiny tire tracks stretch from just below the dune to the water – broken only by footprints.

I follow the tracks back to the wooden walkway and look over my shoulder to see my own footprints on the beach. I want to go back and fill them in, to pack the sand hard and smooth.

But it is time for me to leave and let the water wash away my footprints.

My mom, aunt, and I walk down the road beside the marsh at dusk. We follow a familiar path, stopping only to look at the same old alligator under the popcorn tree and, far away, an egret standing still in the reeds. I imagine that the blue heron is sitting on the post in the creek.

I think about my family back at our beach house. My sisters and cousins are probably in the hammock, swaying back and forth, listening to the grown-ups talk.

I think also about the tiny sea turtles swimming in the ocean. By tomorrow night, they will have found a safe place, nestled among the weeds and currents, where they can float and grow strong.

Someday, many years from now, they too will return to this beach, following their own mysterious trail in the sand.

Learn More About Loggerheads

* The loggerhead turtle became the official reptile for the state of South Carolina in 1988 because of the interest and concern of children and their teachers who worked with their local senator to write and pass legislation that designated the loggerhead as the state reptile.

* The Loggerhead's scientific name is *Carretta carretta*. It is called "loggerhead" because of its large head.

* The loggerhead is one of eight sea turtle species. Five of those species nest in the United States.

* Although the loggerhead has on at least one occasion nested as far north as New Jersey, its primary nesting sites are the beaches and offshore islands in the southeastern United States. Florida alone provides almost 90 percent of the turtle's nesting sites.

* A threatened species, the loggerhead needs our help. Some scientists estimate that only one in 10,000 eggs will become an adult turtle. Only one in about 1,500 hatchlings survives to reproductive age.

* The adult female loggerhead lays around 120 eggs in each nest.

* Some experts believe that a female hatchling imprints the texture, smell and taste of the sand when she first pulls herself across a beach from the nest to the ocean and thus "remembers" the beach where she hatched. Nevertheless, the loggerhead's true navigational ability remains a mystery. Some scientists even think sea turtles locate the beach of their birth through a genetic trait or the geomagnetic field of the earth.

* You can learn even more about the loggerhead and other sea turtles. Ask a grown up to take you to the library and help you find books about marine turtles. Or, visit the following web site: www.cccturtle.org.

SOURCES

Carr, Archie. *The Sea Turtle: So Excellent a Fishe*. Austin: U of Texas P, 1967.

Hopkins-Murphy, Sally R., Charlotte P. Hope, and Margaret E. Hoyle. *A History of Research and Management of the Loggerhead Turtle (Caretta caretta) on the South Carolina Coast: Final Report to the U.S. Fish and Wildlife Service*. Charleston: SC Department of Natural Resources, 1999.

O'Keefe, M. Timothy. *Sea Turtles: The Watcher's Guide*. Lakeland: Larsen's Outdoor Publishing, 1995.

Look Out For Sea Turtles. Pamphlet. Santee Cooper. S.C.

Help Protect Loggerheads

✳ Remind grown ups to turn off beachfront lights after 10 p.m. from May 1 to October 31.

✳ If you go for a walk on the beach at night and see a turtle coming ashore to nest, stay where you are and be very still and quiet. If she gets scared by your movement, she will go back into the ocean without nesting.

✳ If you find a stranded hatchling, place it near the edge of the water. Do not carry it out into the ocean.

✳ Depending on where you live, call the number listed below if you go for an early morning walk and see tracks made by a nesting turtle. The nest might need to be relocated. You should also call if you see someone digging up a nest.

IN FLORIDA:
Florida Fish and Wildlife Conservation Commission
1-800-DIAL-FMP (3425-367) or page staff at (800) 241-4653
(ID#274-4867)
www.state.fl.us/gfc

IN GEORGIA:
Department of Natural Resources
1-912-262-3336
www.dnr.state.ga.us

IN NORTH CAROLINA:
Department of the Environment and Natural Resources/
North Carolina Aquarium Society
1-800-832-FISH
www.aquariums.state.nc.us/files/rehab.htm

IN SOUTH CAROLINA:
Department of Natural Resources
1-800-922-5431
www.dnr.state.sc.us/marine/turtles.html

ADOPT A TURTLE
Contact the Sea Turtle Survival League, c/o Caribbean Conservation Corporation, 4424 NW 13th St., Suite A-1, Gainesville, FL, 32609; call 1-800-678-7853; or visit their web site at www.cccturtle.org.

About PCF Press

PCF Press is the publishing imprint of Palmetto Conservation Foundation. We promote access and appreciation for South Carolina's natural and historical wonders by publishing valuable information about our state.
For inquiries or to order books, visit your local bookseller or our website at: www.palmettoconservation.org

ALSO, FROM PCF PRESS...

The Waterfalls of South Carolina (Second Edition)
This unique guide is an essential exploring companion for every resident or visitor to South Carolina's spectacular mountains. 80 pages, full color photographs and maps. Trade paperback $12.95. ISBN 0-9679016-5-0

A River in Time: The Yadkin-Pee Dee River System
An extraordinary tale of discovery along one of the largest river systems on the East Coast. 200 pages, 50+ full color photographs and maps. Hardcover $39.95. ISBN 0-9679016-3-4.

Behind the Scenes: Sketches of Selected South Carolina First Ladies
The women who have enjoyed the title and privilege of First Lady of South Carolina are a fascinating lot. Featuring personal memoirs, archival photos and genealogical details, Behind the Scenes is an important addition to South Carolina history. 120 pages, 53 B&W photographs. Hardcover $24.95. ISBN 0-9679016-4-2.

The Palmetto Trail: Lowcountry Guide
Part travel planner, part hiking companion, the Lowcountry Guide features anecdotal tales plus a thorough description of the Palmetto Trail's 100+ route in this part of the state. 90 pages, 51 B&W photos, 5 color maps. Wire Binding $12.95. ISBN 0-9679016-2-6.